Flight Down

by Thomas Kingsley Troupe

www.12StoryLibrary.com

12-Story Library is an imprint of Peterson Publishing
Company and Press Room Editions.

Produced for 12-Story Library by Red Line Editorial

Photographs ©: iStockphoto, cover, 3

Cover Design: Laura Polzin

ISBN
978-1-63235-161-6 (hardcover)
978-1-63235-200-2 (paperback)
978-1-62143-252-4 (hosted ebook)

Library of Congress Control Number: 2015934305

Printed in the United States of America
Mankato, MN
June, 2015

CHAPTER
1

I don't really expect anyone to believe any of this. I mean, everyone knows people make crap up all the time to make themselves seem cool or exciting or whatever. Maybe they don't have enough going on in their lives, so they tell crazy stories to prove they're not boring losers.

So, if you don't believe me, I get it.

But what happened to my little sister, Maddie, and me last summer is absolutely true. I still feel the pain in my foot anytime I think about it.

I'm sure everybody heard about Flight 768 on the news. For a while it was all anyone was talking about. It's not exactly the way I planned to become famous or well known or anything.

I'd rather people knew me for being the star of the school basketball team or something.

When it comes down to it, I blame it all on my parents for getting divorced. Really, if they would've stayed together, none of this would've happened.

Seriously, why couldn't they just figure it out and get along?

So, my dad and my mom split up a few years ago. I won't get into it, but it was kind of ugly. There were years of shouting and crying and it was just dumb. Maddie, my sister, did everything she could to try and get them to quit fighting. I just tried my best to ignore it. I mean, it wasn't like they were punching each other in the face or anything, but they said things no one needed to hear—especially their kids. That kind of fighting.

Ultimately, there was nothing either of us could do. They got divorced, and that was the end of it. Then, in a major jerk move, my dad took a new job that moved him from where we lived in Madison, Wisconsin, to Tampa, Florida.

We went from seeing him every other weekend to every summer.

Yeah, awesome!

No, not really. It sucked on so many levels. Before Dad moved, I couldn't wait for the school year to be over so I could relax, hang out with buds, and visit my friend's cabin. We'd hang out down at the lake and act like idiots. But once Dad moved, those days were over. I don't think it affected Maddie as much because she was younger and didn't have any fun summer plans, but it royally ruined my summers. I had to leave my best friends behind. And last year, I had to leave my girlfriend, Vicki, behind, too. She was pretty upset. It took me a while to convince her that we could still be together even though I was going to be gone all summer. We could do the long distance sort of thing. Like that ever works.

So last year was a big deal. I was sixteen, and Maddie was twelve. Mom figured I was old enough to keep an eye on Maddie, so we got to fly out on our own to see Dad in Florida. It was cheaper, and let's face it, much easier for Mom. My dad was the last person she wanted to see after a long flight.

Mom drilled us a million times on where we needed to go and what we needed to do once we got to Dane County Regional Airport. Drop off our bags here, show them our boarding passes, go through the security thing. It was like Mom forgot we'd done this before. We'd been going to stupid Florida for a couple of years already.

When we checked in, I didn't really pay attention to where our seats were. I was actually hoping I wouldn't be seated next to Maddie. I just wanted to do crap on my tablet and not have her bother me. But I knew if I didn't sit next to her, she'd say something to Dad, and I'd get an earful.

Once we were on the plane and heading down the aisle, I saw our row. Sure enough, our seats were right next to each other. I was on the aisle and she was in the middle seat. There was a big guy with a long beard sitting next to the window. He was wearing a T-shirt that looked paper-thin and was covered in sweat stains. Plane seats are pretty uncomfortable as it is, and he looked like he was jammed in there pretty good. He had to be hating life right about then.

Before she even opened her mouth, I knew what Maddie was going to say.

"We need to trade seats, Drew," she whispered.

I was trying to find a spot for my bag in the overhead compartment.

"I asked for the aisle seat," I whispered back. "I shouldn't have to change just because you—"

"I'm *not* sitting next to that guy," Maddie insisted, a little more loudly.

I looked over as Big 'N' Beardy's head tilted up. He had definitely heard her.

"Would you shut up?" I hissed, trying to get her to keep her voice down before things got ugly.

Maddie just widened her blue eyes and stared at me as if to say: *Want me to cause a scene, Drew?*

I didn't.

This is where I should probably say something about my sister. Maddie's always been a complete pain. She's one of those girls who

8

thinks that people exist just to serve her, and that all she needs to do is sit back and wait. And maybe, like, smile every once in a while. She always acted as if she couldn't do a single thing for herself, and if she ever by chance was forced to do something, she complained the entire time. I was amazed she had any friends. Whenever she would have a meltdown, Mom would say, "That's our Maddie, continuing her twelve-year reign of terror."

If I called her a princess, she got mad, but she didn't mind when Dad called her "Daddy's Girl," which made me want to throw up. I guess I should be thankful no one ever called me "Mama's Boy." That would suck.

Anyway, I ended up sitting next to Mr. Big 'N' Beardy. I just needed Maddie to shut up before it got any more awkward.

So, I don't want to sound mean or anything, but this guy was spilling over the sides of his seat and into mine. I couldn't use my left armrest, and I was afraid to put my tray table down.

I watched Maddie sift through her backpack, looking for something. She had her cell phone in one hand and her always-present stick of lip balm in the other.

"No way," she groaned. "No flippin' way."

"What? What now?" I asked while finishing up a text message to Vicki.

If we were going to make this long-distance thing work, I had to be committed, and that meant sending some sappy texts. I had to stay focused. Not to mention, I knew I had to switch my phone to airplane mode at any second.

"My headphones are gone," Maddie whined. "Did you take them?"

"Why would I take your headphones? Yours are garbage."

"I have no idea, but someone took them. They're not in my bag," Maddie said, zipping up her purple backpack and kicking it beneath the seat in front of her. I was just glad they had those metal bars underneath to keep her bag from ending up under the feet of the lady sitting in front of her.

I put my headphones on, desperate to listen to something—anything but her. It was amazing how much better music was to my ears than the sound of her voice.

CHAPTER
2

Knowing even a little about Maddie, it shouldn't surprise anyone that she ended up with the right ear bud while I got the left one. Because that totally happened. The flight attendant offered her some of those cheap airline headphones, but Maddie wasn't having it. Nope. Not good enough for the princess.

I was planning on playing this pretty violent game where you need to defend a fort with a machine gun and Molotov cocktails. It was dumb and bloody, but it made time pass quickly, and it was fun watching things explode. But sure enough, within minutes, Maddie was whining that we should watch a movie.

"I'm not watching any dumb movies about what's-her-name with the bow and arrows," I said.

"Then let's find something we both like," Maddie insisted.

Right. Like that would ever happen. I didn't keep an inventory of chick flicks in my queue just in case my stupid sister left her headphones at home. We started watching a horror movie. I was sure she'd bail within ten minutes, but she didn't. Instead, she asked me so many dumb questions, I couldn't really get into it.

We must've been in the air for two hours when I totally had to pee. I usually don't like to get up during a flight and use those ridiculously small bathrooms, but nature was calling. I handed my tablet to Maddie and slipped past her.

"Where are you going?" Maddie asked, gaping up at me as if I were insane.

"I'm heading to the grocery store," I replied. "Did you want something?"

Maddie raised her eyebrows the way my mom did whenever I said something smart-alecky.

"The bathroom, okay?" I snapped. "Is that all right with you?"

"Don't take too long," Maddie insisted, and sort of motioned to the big guy, who was still staring out the window.

"If I'm not back in five minutes, file a missing person's report."

"You're not even a little bit funny," she said.

I slipped into the aisle, and that's when the plane jerked like we'd hit some sort of speed bump in the clouds. Someone in the seats behind us cried out. Almost immediately, the little *bing-bong* sounds came on. I think it was the seat belt light or whatever.

I put my hand on the seat in front of me to steady myself.

"I'm sorry, sir, you'll have to get back to your seat," said a flight attendant with crunchy-looking blonde hair. "We'll all need to buckle up."

"I just have to use the restroom," I said, as if that would be enough for her to let me through. Truth was, at that moment I didn't feel like I needed to go anymore.

"We're just hitting some turbulence, so please return to your seat. You'll be able to go in a—"

Before she could finish, the plane jerked again. This time, it felt as if a wing had clipped something. More people shouted. An overhead compartment popped open, and a passenger's dingy-looking brown carry-on bag dropped out, falling into the aisle.

I know it's weird, but I remember thinking, *Wow. Even the plane is pooping itself.*

I slipped back into my seat. The guy with the beard was still staring out the window, unaffected by it all. I leaned forward and peered around him, trying to get a look out the window. But I couldn't see anything. It was just a big patch of bright white light.

"This is bad," Maddie said, once I was locked back into my seat belt.

FLIGHT DOWN

In the three seconds I had been gone, she had turned my movie off and was looking through the stuff on my phone. I remember thinking I was going to yell at her later about being such a snoop. It really wasn't the time to do that, just then.

There was another *bing-bong* warning tone, and the pilot came on over the loudspeaker, saying something about hitting a rough patch. He didn't sound like he believed it himself, but it's not like he was just going to come out and say, "Well, folks, this is the big one. I hope you're okay with whomever or whatever you worship, 'cause we're going down."

"This plane is going to crash," Maddie whispered.

"Would you shut up?" I whispered back. I didn't want her to freak people out for no reason—one of those people being me.

As if to keep us good and scared, the plane shook again. The lights in the cabin went off for a full two seconds and then flickered on again. Outside, I heard the engines grinding like they were in pain. There was a sound like a metal can being torn open, and those little yellow oxygen masks dropped down in front of us.

"Oh no! Drew!" Maddie shrieked, grabbing my arm. "This can't be happening!"

I saw there were tears in her eyes. She grabbed the yellow cone and strapped it onto her face. I put mine on, too, feeling the cool oxygen flowing into the mask, just like the flight attendant said it would during her corny little demo before the flight. I don't remember doing it, but apparently I felt the need to hold my sister's hand. At least that's what she says when she tells this story.

The plane shook again, jostling us good and hard. I looked over and saw that the big guy hadn't moved. He hadn't even bothered to put his oxygen mask on. He just stared straight ahead. It was like he was frozen in fear or something.

"Hey man," I said, my voice muffled by the mask. I tapped him on his beefy shoulder. "You should—"

The last thing I remember was hearing what sounded like a huge metallic groan, and then there was wind. Like an insane gust of wind that wouldn't quit.

People were screaming. Maddie dug her fingers into my arm.

My head slammed into something, and I was out.

CHAPTER
3

I don't know how long I was unconscious. I remember feeling like I'd been run over by a semi truck, knocked flat, and dragged down the road a few miles. I didn't want to open my eyes, since I was pretty sure I was dead.

"Oh. Ow. Ow," said an airy voice next to me. Maddie's voice.

I slowly cracked my eyes open. My eyelids felt almost glued shut. There was a bright light, and I couldn't see a thing for a second or two. I figured I had to be dead. That's what the bright light was, right? When people have a near-death experience, they always talk about how they saw a bright light. I was positive that's what was happening to me.

Then my vision cleared, and I wished I had kept my eyes shut.

There was wreckage everywhere. The seats in front of me, where I remembered a couple of ladies had been sitting, were torn to shreds. Actually, most of the plane in front of me was gone, so I was staring outside. I saw twisted hunks of metal all over the place. There were pieces jammed into the ground, torn in places and mashed up. One of the giant jet engines was caved in, barely attached to a wing that wasn't attached to anything anymore.

"Drew? I . . . I think I'm in trouble, Drew."

I couldn't look over at Maddie just then. Not yet. She would have to wait. My head was dizzy with what I was seeing. It was too much. It looked like we were out in the middle of nowhere, and there were dead bodies lying everywhere.

I didn't want to think about the bodies. Some of them looked fine, like they were people just taking a nap. The others? I really don't want to think about them. All I can say is the big guy with the beard next to me wasn't staring out the window anymore. There wasn't a window, and he was dead. But he was still strapped into his seat next to me. His heavy, lifeless hand touched my leg. I'd never seen a dead body before then, but I was sitting beside one, and it freaked me out. I swatted his hand away.

Even moving a little bit hurt. I touched my forehead, and it was wet. And sore. When I looked at my fingers, there was blood on them.

"Drew?"

Maddie. What if my sister was all messed up like the other passengers? What if she was bloody, too?

I turned, afraid of what I would see. My little sister looked back at me, her eyes red and wet with tears. She blinked a little, and her face crumpled into a twisted smile. She looked like she was happy, but about to start crying again.

I was too stunned to do anything.

"I thought you were dead," Maddie whispered. Her voice shuddered a bit, and she winced. "When I opened my eyes and saw that everyone else was dead, I thought you were dead, too."

Everyone was dead. That didn't seem possible, so at the time I chose not to believe it. Somehow we had survived the crash, so I figured other people must have survived, too.

"I'm not dead," I remember saying. She fell back into her twisted seat, and I saw something that almost unhinged me.

The blood on her hands. The blood on her shirt.

"I'm hurt, Drew," Maddie said.

Maddie's right hand clutched something. I looked, and realized there was a metal rod sticking out of the right side of her belly. The part I could see was about the length of a ruler, but thicker, sort of square shaped. It looked like someone had jammed a stake into her, like they were trying to kill a vampire but missed the heart by a foot—lucky for Maddie. If it had hit her dead center instead of off to the side, I'd be telling a different story.

I just stared for a second, feeling stunned and helpless.

"It hurts if I try to pull it," Maddie said, whispering as if she were afraid to wake up the dead people around us. "I don't know what to do."

I didn't know either, but I figured yanking the piece of metal out might do more damage than good.

I unbuckled my seat belt. I wasn't sure where I was going or what I thought I could do, but something told me we had to get up. I had to get Maddie some help. I stood up, half expecting to fall over. My head felt swimmy, but I was stable. I helped Maddie unbuckle her seat belt.

That's when the smell hit me.

I didn't know what jet fuel smelled like, but a strong odor hit me just then. I looked and saw the ground was wet with a dark and cloudy liquid that definitely wasn't water.

"Don't touch that thing," I remember saying to Maddie. "We'll get some help. There's got to be someone around here . . ."

I never finished what I had started to say. From where I stood, I saw more horror than I could ever have imagined. Bodies everywhere. And a few yards away, fire.

"Get up, Maddie," I said hurriedly. "Get up! Get up! Get—"

"I can't, Drew," Maddie whined. "It hurts."

"It's going to hurt a whole lot worse if you don't get up!" I shouted, no longer afraid to make noise. I saw the flames spreading across the ground. The smell of fuel and burning plastic filled the air.

As if to get me moving, flames ignited a patch of tall grass. The fire was spreading fast. The whole area would be engulfed soon. And we would be, too, if we didn't move. Like, now.

Maddie shrieked. I pulled her up out of her seat, trying my best not to bump the thing jabbing into her side. Maddie screamed super loud when I lifted her. I didn't blame her one bit. Her wound looked painful.

I threw Maddie's arm around my neck, and we stumbled out of the wreckage as fast as we could. I wasn't sure if we were going to make it. I felt the fire's heat right behind us as flames crackled and burned. We dodged bodies and wreckage as we moved away from the fire.

There was a weird whistling, followed by an explosion behind us.

BOOM!

CHAPTER
4

The blast knocked us off our feet and tossed us to the grassy edge of a swamp. I landed face down in the muck and felt Maddie's knee smack me in the back.

I rolled over and tried to pull myself up. My hands just sank down in the muck. I didn't know where we were, but I knew it was going to be tough going. Maddie was lying on her side and curled up with her hands around the metal bar sticking out of her. I remember thinking: *Oh no, I hope she didn't land on that.* I couldn't imagine the pain she was in.

Maddie wasn't even thirteen yet. The worst injury she'd ever had was when she scraped the crap out of her leg trying to learn how to ride her bike. It was only a little road rash, but she screamed and carried on like she needed to go to the emergency room.

But now, when she really needed to go to the ER, we were stuck in the middle of a swamp, probably hundreds of miles from a hospital. To this day, I still don't know how she was able to handle it.

I used some of the swamp water to wipe the muck off of my face. I turned to find Maddie struggling to sit up. Her shorts were muddy, and there were fresh cuts on her leg. We both just sat and watched the plane wreckage burn for a moment. All of those people. All of that luggage. All of it, just cooking right in front of us like some sort of sad, sick barbeque. I couldn't help thinking of the people who might not know about the crash. They would be waiting at the airport for one of those dead bodies. And how would there even be funerals for all of those people burned to ash?

Just thinking it, even now, makes me feel guilty. Why did Maddie and I survive the crash when nobody else did?

I can't think about it. I don't want to.

I just remember looking around and seeing all of this fire and smoke. Even where we were sitting, at the edge of a swampy puddle, I didn't think we were safe from the spreading flames.

"Are you okay, Maddie?" I asked, knowing she wasn't.

"No," she snapped. "My shorts are all wet. And my legs got all sliced up."

Never mind that big metal rod sticking out of your gut, I remember thinking. I still couldn't stand to look at it, all bloody and just poking out of her. I wondered how sharp that piece of metal was and how much that must be hurting her and how deep it went. Even though I'm no baby, I'm pretty sure I would've been bawling like a newborn, but Maddie seemed over it. *Seriously, was this my helpless little sister?*

"We need to get moving," I said watching the fire carefully. Black smoke was blowing everywhere, stinging our eyes and causing us to cough. The heat from the flames baked my skin a little. Any hope of getting my bags was gone.

We didn't even have one of those stupid little bottles of water they gave us on the plane.

"Shouldn't we stay here and wait for some rescue guys or whatever?"

"We're in the middle of nowhere, there's a fire spreading, and you're looking like a stuck pig."

"Don't call me a pig, Drew," Maddie snapped, and I saw her wince. She was suffering, but she was trying hard not to show it.

"You know what I mean," I shot back. I reached into my wet jeans pocket and found my cell phone.

My cell phone!

I stood up with a groan and pushed the home button. Nothing. Not even a flicker of life. The screen wasn't cracked or anything, but the phone was wet. The stupid thing was useless.

"What, were you going to call for help?" Maddie asked.

I wanted to shoot back a smart-alecky reply, like "No, I was going to order us a pizza. What do you want on your half?" But I didn't have it in me. I just nodded. Maybe it was a dumb idea, thinking my phone could save us. Considering we couldn't see anything but swampland and low brush in every direction, even if my phone had been working, I doubted I would get any sort of signal.

"Maybe mine works," Maddie said. She cried out as she reached for something that wasn't there anymore. "Oh! It was in my backpack, so—"

"So now it's melted," I finished. "And we will be too if we don't move."

"Where are we going to go?"

Truth was, I didn't know. I had no idea where we were or how long it would take for any sort of rescue team to come and find us. I only knew that if I saw what was left of our plane, I'd assume everyone was dead.

But as I looked at the flaming wreckage and hunks of metal spread all over the swampy grassland, I realized something. What was burning in front of us wasn't the entire plane. It couldn't be. It looked like only half of it.

Where was the rest of Flight 768?

"Let's go," I said. I knew I hadn't answered her question, but I also didn't want us to be burned alive.

"What's the point?" Maddie asked. "Are we just going to wander around out in the middle of nowhere until we die?"

"Maddie, we didn't survive a plane crash just to die in some stupid swamp. We'll just walk until we find a road or something."

Only later did I find out we had crashed smack dab in the middle of the Okefenokee National Wildlife Refuge. The whole thing is somewhere around 600 square miles of swampland. But at the time, I didn't know how far we were from civilization. I just knew that we had to move to survive.

I got my sister to her feet, even though she complained and cried out a bunch of times—I didn't blame her. Maddie had just been impaled, for crying out loud. I tried to act confident, but as we started walking, I doubted myself. *Maybe Maddie is right,* I thought. *Maybe we should stay close to the wreckage so the rescue workers can find us.* But then, looking at Maddie's wound, I thought, *What if the rescue workers come too late?*

I had to get help for Maddie, and soon.

FLIGHT DOWN

It was then that I looked up and saw the plume of smoke rising in the distance.

CHAPTER
5

If there was a column of black smoke rising in the distance, it was probably coming from the rest of the plane, right? That's what I thought, anyway. I had no idea how far away it was, but I figured there was a chance that someone else had survived. If so, maybe one of the other survivors could help us. Maybe by some miracle one of them was a doctor who could remove the metal thing from my sister and patch her up.

Anything was better than standing around, waiting for a rescue team that might never show up or a fire to burn us up like it had everyone else.

Maddie thought I was dumb for wanting to walk even farther into the swampy wilderness. She kept insisting we should head back.

"Just shut up, would you?" I snapped. I know, it wasn't cool of me to say that to someone who could likely die at any minute. But really, after a while she got to me. I was just trying my best to get us out of there.

✦ ✦ ✦ ✦ ✦

I kept glancing up to the sky as we picked our way through the brush and tall grass. I didn't really expect a rescue team to show up right away, but I was hopeful. At one point I turned around and looked back at the wreckage of burning plane we had left behind.

It didn't look as if the fire was spreading, but I still thought heading toward the distant smoke was the best idea. Even if the smoke wasn't coming from another part of the plane, it had to be a sign of life. Maybe someone lived out there and maybe they had a car or a phone or something to help us.

As we walked, the ground under my feet felt marshy, and I was hit with a sudden and terrifying thought. Alligators. There were alligators down south. Heck, one of the college teams in Florida had an alligator for a mascot. I stopped in my tracks. Maddie stopped, too.

"We're not even close," Maddie said. "Are we going to turn around?" She had her hand on the piece of metal. It looked like she'd just finished stabbing herself and was still holding the handle of the dagger.

"I just thought of something," I said. "And you won't like it."

"Oh, worse than being stabbed and lost in the middle of nowhere? Worse than being in a plane crash?"

I looked at her hand. She'd washed it off in the water back in the swamp, but now it was covered in blood again. She was still bleeding. Why she wasn't unconscious or even groggy was beyond me. I don't know. I just remember being amazed at how well she was doing, all things considered.

"Alligators," I said. "I'm pretty sure there are some out here."

That bit of news seemed to knock the wind out of her a bit. As if she needed another shot to the stomach. I saw her breathing change. She was panicking, and I was pretty sure she would start hyperventilating any second. Even so, she was as Maddie as ever.

"I told you this was stupid," she said. "If we had stayed closer to the wreck, they'd stay away. A crocodile wouldn't want to be near fire. Animals are afraid of fire, right?"

I shrugged. How would I know?

"I'm not a survival expert," I shouted. "I don't even know anything about crocodiles or alligators or whatever else might want to kill us out here, okay? I'm just trying to get you help."

"Well, you're doing a terrible job," Maddie whispered.

"You want to go back? Fine. Go!" I shouted.

That probably wasn't one of my proudest moments, sending my stabbed and bleeding twelve-year-old sister off on her own into a potentially alligator-infested swamp, I have to admit.

"Maybe I should," Maddie said. "You don't know what you're doing. Mom always says you never think before you act. This is proof."

"Yeah? Well, it's easy for you to say," I snapped back. "Everyone does everything for you. You just need to act helpless and let everyone else take care of your problems."

"That's not true!" Maddie said.

I could tell she was getting upset.

"At least I'm trying to do something," I said. "You just . . ."

Maddie turned away from me, and I was pretty sure she was crying. It didn't make me feel good to say that stuff to her. Not even a little bit. But still, I was doing the best I could.

I didn't say anything but just kept walking toward the smoke. I wasn't sure if she would follow me, or even if she could, but I kept going. I was about to turn around when I heard the squishing sound of her footsteps behind me.

Would I have left my wounded sister behind to die all by herself? No, of course not. I'm not that big of a jerk, despite what she says. Or what I've said. Maybe heading toward the

37

smoke wasn't the best idea, but really, how was I supposed to know? They don't teach this stuff in school.

✦ ✦ ✦ ✦ ✦

We walked for what felt like hours, not really saying much. I noticed the ground was getting wetter, and my legs were starting to feel heavier with each step. Maddie was leaning on me more and more.

"How much farther?" Maddie asked.

I had no idea how to answer my sister, but I stopped to look at the smoke on the horizon. It didn't seem like we were any closer. I looked back in the direction we'd come and saw the smoke from the wreckage we'd left behind. We were still closer to our crash site. At the speed we were going, it was going to take us forever to get to the other crash site.

"I have to go potty," Maddie declared.

"Well, go. No one's stopping you," I said. It probably sounded a lot more smart-alecky than I meant it.

Maddie went off and hid behind some tall grass for privacy, but I turned around anyway.

"Watch for gators, Drew," she called.

"I will," I promised.

A second later, I heard her cry out in pain. I ran toward her, afraid one of them had gotten her.

"What're you doing?" she screamed. "Get out of here! I'm peeing!"

"You screamed."

"I'm squatting down with a metal bar jammed into my belly," Maddie cried. "It hurts, okay?"

"Okay, okay," I said and turned around. As I caught my breath, I heard something in the distance.

It sounded like salvation. Like a helicopter off in the distance.

CHAPTER
6

I don't know why, but I almost couldn't believe it. I mean, at that point I should have been ready to believe just about anything, right? We had survived a plane crash, narrowly missed being blown up in an explosion, and my sister was still alive, even with a metal rod sticking out of her gut.

But a helicopter? In the sky? It was just too unbelievable right then.

"Maddie," I shouted. "Get up. Get up!"

"I hear it. I hear it!"

I couldn't wait for her to finish whatever was taking her so long. I ran out toward the sound. I waved my hands like some sort of lunatic, back and forth like I've seen actors do in

TV shows where they're stranded on an island or whatever and see a ship off in the distance.

I couldn't see the helicopter yet, with the trees all around us, but I waved anyway, looking up into the sky. I remember thinking: *This is it. This is how we're going to be rescued.*

I figured they'd fly us out of that never-ending stretch of swampy nature and get us down to Tampa. We could get my sister some help, and I could get a dry pair of socks.

It's weird. Until then, I had forgotten about the blood I'd found on my head earlier. I realized maybe they should look at that, too.

"Maddie, c'mon!" I shouted.

I remember thinking that they were going to land real quick and snatch me up, and if she didn't hurry, she was going to get left behind. But then I scanned the sky and saw that the helicopter was farther away than I had thought—way off on the horizon.

"We have to move!" I screamed. "They're not going to see us!"

Maddie ran toward me, wincing with every step. I noticed for the first time in however many

41

hours that she really didn't look too good. Her face was pale. In her own words, she looked "like death."

The helicopter was one of those smaller ones that always remind me of a dragonfly. You know, the kind that have a big bubble up front where the pilot sits and a long tail. I kept my eye on it as it zipped along the horizon, and then started running as fast as I could in its direction, screaming and shouting. I didn't even look to see if Maddie was following me. I had to catch the pilot's attention.

All I could think was, *if we want to survive this crap, we need to get on that copter.*

"Drew!"

I heard Maddie shouting from behind, but I didn't stop. I kept running. My head felt a little off, like maybe I wasn't in any condition to be running. But it didn't matter. The pilot had to see me. Then I could show him where my sister was, and we'd be home free.

Well, we'd be in Tampa, anyway. Not really the same thing as home, but good enough. Better than a swamp.

After a few more steps, I realized why Maddie was shouting. Without watching where I was going, I had run headlong into a deeper swamp. In one step, I was on squishy ground. The next, I was up to my waist in filthy water. My foot sunk deep into the muck. I wasn't going any farther.

"Hey! Here!" I shouted, still waving my hands.

I splashed around desperately, still hoping to catch the pilot's attention. Noticing the direction it was headed, I realized the helicopter was probably going to our crash site. The smoke from the wreckage we had left behind was still rising into the sky. The pilot wasn't bothering to look for survivors out where we were.

I hated to admit it, but Maddie probably was right. We should've stayed where we were.

"Get out of there!" Maddie screamed.

She was about halfway to the point where I'd stupidly stepped into the swamp, but was moving much slower than I had. Her hand was curled around the metal rod as she headed my way, maybe to keep it from moving and hurting her even more.

I was whistling, screaming at the top of my lungs, shouting at the disappearing copter. As I did, flocks of little birds flew up from the tall grass and headed for the sky.

The helicopter was gone without even any sort of hint that it had seen or heard me. I watched it disappear in the distance as if I'd been imagining the dumb thing the whole time.

Idiots, I thought. *You just flew past the only survivors!*

I looked, and Maddie was just getting to where I was. She slowed down and stood at the edge of the water. She looked worn out, defeated, as though she was about to drop any second. She looked at me.

"Are you stuck?"

I shook my head, even though I wasn't completely sure. I mean, I had been so busy trying to flag down the helicopter that I hadn't thought about getting out of the swamp. I tried pulling my foot up, and the mud seemed to pull back at my shoe. I knew if I wasn't careful, I would lose the stupid thing.

"You should get out of there, Drew," Maddie whispered. "Like, now."

She looked out past me, over to the opposite edge of the swamp, and it creeped me out. Especially with her looking like she did, all almost dead and stuff.

As I wheeled around, scanning the still waters, I felt panic rise up through my body. It started down at my feet, rose into my gut, and ran up through my arms. I swore I could see the reeds along the edge of the swamp swaying as if something were moving slowly toward me.

You didn't have to be a genius to figure out what that something might be.

As I carefully pulled one of my feet free of the murky bottom, I looked across the water. There was this greenish stuff along the surface. There were a couple of pieces of floating wood, partially sunk beneath the surface.

It didn't seem like there was anything else in the swamp with me. At least, that's what I was thinking until I saw one of the "logs" dip below the surface of the water.

If I was scared before, I was pretty much crapping my pants right then and there.

CHAPTER
7

I probably mentioned that I didn't know a whole heck of a lot about alligators, but I do now. The only thing I knew at that moment was: *There's one in the swamp with me.*

I tried to swim, but one of my feet was still stuck in the muck. I tried to kick myself loose with my foot as best as I could, but I wasn't getting free fast enough. I saw ripples gliding across the top of the murky waters, breaking up that green stuff floating on top.

I heard Maddie crying out, too. She screeched, "Hurry! Hurry!" a couple of times, and when I turned my attention to her for a second, I saw she was pointing at the ripply spot in the swamp. It was coming for me, and I needed to get out of the water and fast.

With everything I had left in the tank, I pulled my foot up and felt something give. My foot was free. I'd left my shoe behind, and it was an expensive shoe, too, but who really cares? What good are shoes if you don't have anything to put in them? With my feet free, I swam like I was going for the gold medal or something. I got swamp water in my eyes and mouth, but I didn't care about that either.

Maddie bent over like she was going to haul me out of the water, but I swatted her hand away. I didn't need her using whatever energy she had left to help me. Besides, couldn't alligators smell blood, and didn't that just make them hungrier? Or was that sharks?

I scrambled out of the water, clawing at the grass in an effort to pull myself out. One foot had a shoe on it, the other covered in a soggy sock. I flipped onto my back and crept backward, crablike, watching the water. I think I half-expected a gigantic alligator to lurch up and swallow both Maddie and me whole.

The only glimpse we got of the thing was the top of its head as it rose up from under the water. It sort of looked at us with its shiny, black eyes. I wondered if it was trying to decide whether it should bother with us or not.

"Keep moving back," I whispered. "It might come after us."

For like the first time I could ever remember, Maddie didn't argue. She took a few careful steps back. I guess if the alligator had made a move I would've gotten to my feet and ran like my pants were on fire. I remembered thinking: *Alligators have short legs. There's no way something built like that could catch us.*

Like I said, I pretty much didn't know anything about those dumb things before that day.

"You lost your shoe," Maddie said breathlessly. I could barely hear her over the sound of my heart beating against my ribs.

"I could've lost a lot more," I whispered back, still slowly making my way backward. For some reason, I didn't dare stand up. I thought any sudden moves might startle the alligator and give it another reason to come after me.

Maddie didn't say anything, but she watched as I slowly crawled back a bit more.

I didn't dare turn away from the creepy bubble eyes watching us from the swamp. Now that I think about it, there could've been other alligators roaming around in the grass nearby, just as hungry and just as dangerous.

We truly were a couple of dumb, lucky city kids who had no idea what we were doing out in the middle of a living, breathing pile of nature.

When I was a good ten yards or so away from the edge of the swamp, I slowly got to my feet. I had been in a staring contest with the alligator the whole time, ready to run if it decided to go for the first down.

I had no idea how big that sucker was, but I must've looked like too much trouble for it. It disappeared beneath the dark water as if it had been some nightmarish vision. I don't know if I had been holding my breath the whole time, but I let out the mother of all sighs as if I'd just narrowly escaped death. Which, you know, I guess I had. Again.

I felt like a dishrag: wet and smelly. My clothes were soaked. Slogging along in the hot and humid air, I felt, for lack of a better word, swampy. It had been bad enough walking through the wilderness after being beat up from the crash. But now, sopping wet and with only one shoe, it was even worse.

Of course, I took a look at my sister and felt like the biggest wimp of all time. She had it much worse than I did.

"Still want to head toward the smoke?" Maddie asked.

I nodded. I didn't think going back the way we had come made much sense. From the looks of it, the helicopter had finished circling that area already. Meanwhile, the front end of the plane was probably off in the distance where that smoke was coming from, who knew how many miles away. I figured the helicopter would go there next. If I remembered right, the front end of the plane was where those black box recorders and stuff were, and I figured they would be looking for those things to investigate the cause of the crash.

Maddie and I headed off, moving more slowly than ever through the marshy wilderness. I didn't want to think about it, but it didn't seem we were getting any closer to that beacon of hope off in the distance.

I was hungry, thirsty, and miserable. I thought about my girlfriend, Vicki. I wondered if the news of our crash was on TV yet. Maybe she was crying and figuring I was dead or whatever. My mom was probably feeling like garbage, too. She had sent her kids off on a plane by themselves and look what happened.

My dad probably felt pretty crappy, too.

I remember thinking that maybe their grief over thinking they'd lost their two kids would be something that could bring them back together. I'm old enough to know it was a dumb idea, but when you're walking in silence through a whole lot of nothing, your head gets full of dumb thoughts. Wishes, too.

At one point I thought about what might happen if Maddie and I survived but were never found. Would we become some sort of weird nature freaks? Like turn into primitive people who eat dirt and build grass huts? Maybe we'd even learn to hunt alligators and birds with sticks and spears.

Dumb, I know. It was best to just keep walking.

I had no idea how many hours went by, but we walked for a long time. Neither of us talked much. We didn't dare mention it, but we could both see that the sun was going down. It wouldn't be long before we were lost in the dark.

CHAPTER
8

It got to the point where I couldn't even see the smoke off in the distance anymore. It just blended into the darkening sky. If I were the type of guy who gets into sunsets and rainbows and crap, I would've said it was kind of pretty. Maddie beat me to it, though.

"Wow, it's beautiful," she said, stopping to gaze at the dropping sun. We were in a kind of prairie now, with all kinds of tall grass.

"Yeah, but it'll be pitch black in like thirty minutes, I'm guessing."

"So what does that mean?" Maddie looked at me, expecting that I had a plan for what would come next.

I didn't.

"It means we can't really go anywhere," I said. "We won't be able to follow the smoke, and wandering around in the dark could get us killed."

"Oh," Maddie said.

I noticed then how dim her eyes seemed. I had never really seen her as much more than an annoying little sister before that day, but all of a sudden it was sort of like I saw her differently. I thought of her as being something—someone—important to me and noticed that the life in her eyes was fading. That probably doesn't make much sense, but that's what I thought at the time.

To make matters worse, the ground was especially swampy where we were, which made me nervous. Who knew what would be crawling around here in the dark?

There were a few trees that didn't look like anything we had back in Wisconsin. The branches were low and sort of crooked, growing in weird directions. Not like back home, where trees just kind of grew . . . up.

At least there was some good news. It didn't look like Maddie was bleeding anymore.

But then, I didn't know if that was because the wound was scabbing over and somehow healing itself around the metal rod, or if maybe something worse was happening, like it was swollen up and infected.

We stood there for a few minutes, afraid to even sit down. We both watched the sun move lower in the sky, igniting the clouds with a grand splash of orange, red, and purple. The few trees in the distance were like shadows.

It reminded me of a movie I saw when I was a kid—*The Lion King*. That animated one where the lion and all of the animals sing and stuff? I think it was supposed to be in Africa. Right then, I felt like I was in Africa, just waiting for some sort of animal to pounce on us. So I tried to think about them breaking into song instead.

I heard something rustle in the tall grass nearby, and I nearly jumped out of my pants. Maddie turned suddenly, too.

"We have to get out of here," she said.

I can't tell you how many times we said that during our ordeal. Maybe somewhere in the thousands? It seemed like anytime one of us mentioned how hungry, thirsty, or miserable we were, the other one followed up with, "We have to get out of here."

She was right, though. Even if we couldn't leave the swampy wonderland we'd discovered, we'd have to find a safe spot for the night. I eyeballed the trees nearby. They were our best option.

I'm a pretty athletic guy, but my sister isn't. She's in decent shape and everything, but the idea of sports or doing anything that makes you sweaty just isn't her thing. Trying to get a twelve-year-old girl with a serious wound up into a tree is not easy. I managed to get her up on a sturdy branch without too much screaming. That meant we were about four feet off the ground. Luckily, alligators have short legs.

Maddie and I watched the last sliver of sun dip below the horizon. It was so dark within minutes that we couldn't see each other. Neither of us said anything for a little bit. I was too worried about slipping off the branch, breaking my head open, and feeding the bloodthirsty wildlife.

"Are you going to sleep?" Maddie asked.

"I don't think so," I said. "I'm worn out, but there's no way I could sleep up here."

"Good," Maddie whispered with a shuddering sigh. "I'm afraid to."

"You afraid of falling?"

"No," she said and then waited a little bit before adding, "I'm afraid I won't wake up."

Here's where I admit to something: I was glad it was super dark just then, because I cried a little bit. I mean, most of the time I couldn't stand Maddie, but that didn't mean I wanted her dead. She was my little sister, after all. My mom has pictures of me holding Maddie when she was born. In the pictures, I'm grinning like she's the greatest thing in the world. I don't think I ever smile like that anymore. Not like I did in those pictures.

"We're going to get home," I said, once I had a grip on myself and was sure I wouldn't sound like a blubbering baby. I wiped my eyes with my swampy-smelling sleeve and took a deep breath. "One way or another."

"Yeah, maybe," Maddie said. "Well, if we don't make it, I hope you know I love you."

"What?" I said. "Why would you say something like that?"

"I don't know," Maddie said. "You never know what's going to happen. I don't want the last thing I say to you to be something stupid."

I wondered if she knew she was going to die or something. Like maybe she didn't want to worry me. But her saying she loved me didn't help. I think it actually made things worse.

Right then and there I wished I could just pick her up and sprint across this stupid swamp to wherever the rescue team was. But then I had this awful helpless feeling, knowing that there was nothing I could do.

"Don't say crap like that," I said. I knew it wasn't the right thing to say, but I didn't want us to sit in a tree crying like a couple of scared kids. I wanted us to believe we could survive. "You're not going to die," I added.

"Okay, Drew," she whispered. "Sorry."

CHAPTER
9

We were too afraid to sleep or even talk much. Every time we heard some weird noise off in the distance, we both froze up, as if whatever was out there was hunting for us. I'll be the first to admit I was scared to death. I really began to wonder if I was ever going to see my parents or Vicki again. I didn't even know if I would live to see the sun rise.

At one point, I must have dozed for a bit and mumbled something. I don't remember, but apparently I did.

"What did you just say?" Maddie whispered in the dark. I couldn't see her face, but she sounded weary.

"I didn't say anything," I whispered. I felt a little bit out of it. Sitting in a tree for hours like some sort of smelly monkey can do that to a guy.

"It sounded like you said 'Vicki,'" Maddie said.

"I don't know," I muttered. I was worn out. I was hungry enough to eat my arm. If the dumbest thing I did was to whisper my long-distance girlfriend's name, then I was fine with that.

"She's going to dump you, you know," Maddie said, as if it were no big deal.

"What are you talking about?"

"Sometime this summer. She's going to do it. I heard her talking to Claire in the bathroom right before school let out."

I heard Maddie groan as she shifted her weight on the branch, but just then I didn't feel all that sorry for her. I was angry.

"Not that I believe a single word you're saying," I fired back. "But what did she say, exactly?"

Maddie sighed as if it were a huge bother to have to tell me. Just a few hours earlier, she had been saying she loved me and all that stuff. Now it was like she was trying to cut my heart out.

"Well?" I asked sharply, forgetting for a moment that we'd been trying to stay quiet. "What did she say?"

Maddie sighed heavily and continued, "I was in a stall, and I heard her and Claire blabbing about whatever. At one point Claire just flat out asked Vicki what she was going to do about you."

Now I was freaking out. *Claire wanted to know what Vicki was going to do about me? Like what, I'm some sort of problem Vicki has to deal with?*

"And?"

"Well, I know, it sucks, but she said she was just going to wait until after you were in Florida for a little while, and then, you know . . ."

No, I didn't know, but I thought about it. Would she really just dump me? Over the phone? Or even worse, in a text message? The weight of my dead phone in my pocket felt extra heavy. Was there already a text from her waiting out there somewhere? Maybe a response to the message I sent her on the plane?

I miss you already. We can make this work.
Love, D.

I'd never really had a girlfriend before. Vicki was my first. It wasn't because I didn't like girls—I did—but I just had never bothered before. Our relationship sort of happened by accident. A group of us started hanging out, and Vicki and I ended up together. But later it became more than that. I really wanted us to work through this long-distance stuff. I wanted her to be there waiting for me at the airport when I returned home.

So she didn't want to wait around for me. Didn't want to spend the summer hanging on the phone when she could find some other boyfriend who would actually be there for her. Couldn't say I blamed her. Even so . . .

"I'm sorry," Maddie whispered. "Are you okay?"

"I don't want to talk about it," I said.

"Are you mad at me?" she asked. "I thought I should say something, but I just didn't know how to bring it up."

FLIGHT DOWN

I felt stupid. And I know that after everything I'd been through up to that point, it probably seems dumb that I got so upset about my stupid girlfriend or whatever. I mean, I obviously had bigger problems to worry about.

✦ ✦ ✦ ✦ ✦

After what seemed like an eternity, the sun started to rise. My whole body felt rigid and weird from being up in a tree for so long. I looked down below us to see if there were any alligators or any other horrible things lurking in the grass.

When I was sure the coast was clear, I dropped down. My legs didn't want to cooperate, and I fell in a heap. Some sort of giant bug skittered away, and a bunch of birds chittered in the distance.

Once I got to my feet, I looked up at Maddie. It didn't take a med student to see that she was in bad shape. There were dark circles around her eyes, and her hand was caked with dried blood. I didn't want to think about what was going on with her wound. Inside, you know. We just needed to head toward the smoke and . . .

I almost dropped to my knees, as if the fight had been beaten out of me in the twelfth round.

"No," I whispered. "No, no, no . . ."

"Help me down, Drew," Maddie said.

I heard the panic rise in her throat. She could tell that I was upset about something, and I was supposed to be the strong one right now. I was the one who was supposed to keep us going.

But I was about to give up. I didn't know what else to do. I was completely and utterly disoriented.

"What?" Maddie cried. "What is it?"

I turned and looked all around us. The sun was coming up now in the east, which made the opposite direction west. Before the sun set last night, we had been heading southeast.

Or had we?

The smoke had been a beacon for us to follow. It was going to lead us to the rest of the plane. That was really the only option we had, especially since the helicopter had passed right by us.

There was only one problem. The smoke? It was gone.

CHAPTER
10

I reached up and helped lower my
sister to her feet. I felt her tense up, as
though the metal rod jammed in her gut had
shifted and hurt her. I don't think she believed
me when I told her about the smoke not being
there anymore.

Maddie stood there for a second and looked
off where she thought it should be. I pointed
in another direction, toward what I thought
was southeast.

"It was actually over there," I said, quietly.

Maddie put a hand to her face, and I could
hear her begin to cry. She shuddered a little bit
and then buried her whole face in her hands. It
was something she had done since pretty much
forever. Maddie always hid her face when she

cried, as if she was embarrassed or something. Once, a long time ago, when she was just a little kid, I asked her why she did that. She said, "I'm ugly when I cry."

Back when Mom and Dad were screaming at each other constantly, she hid her face a lot. I tried lying to make her feel better, telling her not to be so dumb, that our parents weren't getting divorced; they were just going through a tough time.

This time I just stood there like an awkward jerk, unsure what to do. We were doomed, and I didn't know if I had it in me to lie to her again.

"Don't cry," I said, even though I felt like blubbering right along with her. "C'mon, Maddie."

"It's over," she gasped from behind her hands. She drew in a shuddering breath and let it out. "I'm going to bleed to death. You'll get eaten. That will be the end of us."

I ran my hands across my face and through my filthy hair. I scanned our surroundings, half expecting the smoke to just sort of show up again, like, "Just kidding! Head over this way, kids!"

It didn't.

"If you were going to bleed to death, you would be dead by now," I said.

I'd seen quite a few movies where people got stabbed or shot in the stomach and it seemed like they all died pretty much right away. Maybe they had time to make a final speech or something, but they sure didn't go wandering around for an entire night and then keel over the next day. Plus, I reasoned, it looked like the metal rod had probably missed any important organs. I mean, she was still walking around, right? So how bad could it be?

"Is that supposed to make me feel better?" she demanded, pulling her hands away to look at me.

"Look," I said. "We're alive now, but we're not going to make it if we stand around screaming at each other."

"What's the point? We should've been dead with everyone else on that plane anyway. No one's going to look for us. They'll never know we're alive."

She paused for a moment as if to gather her thoughts.

"Why did we survive, anyway?" she asked finally. "Who decided that all of those other people should die, and we'd just get to wander around in this alligator-infested swamp?"

I shrugged. I didn't have a good answer at the time, and even now, I don't actually have a clue. But that didn't stop me from opening my mouth anyway.

"We're alive for a reason," I said.

"Really?" Maddie asked, wiping her eyes with her dirty hands. "Why, then?"

"We're alive because—we just are," I snapped, feeling myself lose patience. "We can stand around here and cry about it, or we can try to get ourselves rescued. I don't know about you, but I know what I'm going to do."

I set off in the direction I was pretty sure was southeast, where I thought I'd seen the smoke before we hid ourselves up a tree. The ground was wet, and the sock on my shoeless foot was instantly soaked again. I was almost ready to tear the stupid thing off.

"You're going the wrong way," Maddie said finally, clearing her throat.

I kept walking. When I didn't hear her wet footsteps behind mine, I turned. She was just standing there.

"Seriously, Drew," she said.

I didn't say anything, thinking that would get her to drop it and just come along. We were already wasting too much time. I knew we could've been that much closer if she had just kept her mouth shut and followed me.

Maddie didn't budge.

"Do you want me to leave you behind?" I threatened.

Now, for the record, there was no way I was going to leave my sister behind, okay?

"We need to go that way," Maddie insisted, pointing in another direction.

It didn't seem right, and it took everything I had not to argue with her again. But this was my stubborn sister we were talking about, and

I could see she wasn't having it any other way. Plus, it was because of me that we were trekking through this stupid swamp in the first place. So I felt it was her turn to choose what to do. That didn't mean I was happy about it, though.

"Fine," I said and kicked through the grass as I headed the way she wanted to go. "If we get lost, don't scream at me."

Maddie nodded and walked toward me. I slowed my pace a bit so she could catch up.

We walked for hours through the tall, sharp grass. I didn't even want to think about what was out there. At one point, a snake slid across her foot, and she screamed. Without even thinking about it, I kicked it away.

"You just saved my life," Maddie whispered.

"Probably not," I said, trying hard not to show how rattled I'd been by what I'd just done. I was now Drew Rafferty, Snake Kicker. "It probably wasn't even poisonous."

Of course, I was just being modest. I had no idea if that thing was poisonous or venomous or whatever.

"Still. Thanks," Maddie said.

"You're . . ." I began as we crested a small marshy mound. Looking around, I saw a welcome sight.

That is, if you can call a crash site a welcoming sight.

Off in the distance, I saw people. Real, live people. They were tiny, like little yellow action figures or something. They were wearing helmets. There were crates and trucks and another one of those helicopters. I could see the people swarming around chunks of wreckage like hungry ants around a dropped piece of hot dog. Some of them were spraying what looked like white steam around the site.

"We made it," I said, pulling Maddie up to join me.

We were standing in front of a long, muddy trench that cut through the swamp, leading right to where the front part of the plane had ended its journey.

I smiled, wondering if maybe some other passengers really had survived. Seeing people working at the site gave me hope. It even put a smile on my poor sister's face. She shielded her eyes from the blazing midday sun to get a better look.

"I knew it," she said, following me into the muddy trench. We were getting out of there.

CHAPTER
11

We ran as fast as our injuries and exhaustion would allow. I was up ahead a few yards, never taking my eyes off the tiny yellow figures moving around the crash site. I didn't want the rescue workers to be like those mirages thirsty dudes see out in the desert. I would have lost it if they had just disappeared before my eyes. When I was satisfied they weren't just visions on the swampy horizon, I slowed down and waited for Maddie to catch up.

"I'm not sure I want to get into a helicopter, Drew," Maddie said. "I don't want to go into the air again."

I hadn't thought about that. I mean, we *had* just dropped out of the sky less than a day ago. Was I really all that excited to have some tiny machine fly us somewhere? I shook it off and knew when it came down to it, Maddie would, too.

"We need to get you help," I said. "You can't have some piece of metal sticking out of you forever."

Maddie didn't say anything, and that was fine. I didn't want to get into what would likely be the world's most ridiculous argument. We needed saving. Sometimes you don't get to choose how that happens.

The mud was thicker the closer we got. The swamp had filled in the trench up ahead, turning it into a plane-made lake of sorts, which made me wonder whether following the trench to the crash site had been my smartest move.

As we got closer, I started shouting. I think a couple of the workers saw me because they looked up from whatever they were doing and pointed our way.

"They see us!" I shouted.

Suddenly my damp, swampy-smelling clothes didn't seem so heavy. My shoeless foot didn't feel so raw and sore. The throbbing in my head stopped for a second. Maddie and I were going to make it. The people there were real, and they knew we were there.

I saw a couple of the figures in the yellow coveralls start to run toward us. They were maybe two football fields away. I was about to turn to Maddie and let her know they'd seen us, when I heard her scream at the top of her lungs.

"Drew! No!"

I turned around, half expecting her to say something else about the helicopter, but this was different. Behind her, moving fast, was a big, muddy alligator.

The thing looked like a monster. I could see the shiny black eyes on the top of its head. It was almost completely covered in mud, nearly camouflaged in the trench. The thing had to have been at least eight feet long. It glided through the muck and was headed right for Maddie.

I looked around. We were trapped in the trench with nowhere to go. I didn't know how fast the thing could move, but the only way out was up.

"Hurry, Maddie," I shouted. I grabbed her roughly, not really thinking about her injury. "You have to get out of the trench, now."

I struggled in the mud to get some decent footing but was able to boost her up over the edge of the trench. She screamed in pain, but I kept pushing her up until I saw her scrabble her way up into the sloppy grass.

"Drew!" she gasped. "What about you? How are you going to get out?"

I hadn't thought about it, and I didn't have time. There was no way she'd be able to pull me up. I was too heavy, and she was too badly hurt. The only thing I could do was run. I turned and headed toward the wreck. But in that thick muck, running was not exactly what I was doing. I was lumbering forward, more like a zombie than a live person. Ahead of me, I saw the workers wading through the water to get to us. They were still too far away.

I looked over my shoulder and saw the alligator. It wasn't struggling with the water and mud like I was. The thing was right on my tail, maybe five or six feet away. I never should've looked behind me. It was probably one of the dumbest things I'd done on a long list of dumb things. My sopping, shoeless foot sunk into a watery mudhole, and I went down, landing on my side.

I was stuck, and the alligator was on me instantly.

CHAPTER
12

With my shoe-protected foot, I kicked, catching the alligator right in the mouth. The alligator made a rumbling noise that sounded like a clogged garbage disposal. It hissed and came at me again.

I was dead, and I knew it. The yellow rescue dudes wouldn't get to me in time. They'd save my sister and have to pick up whatever scraps of me the alligator left behind.

That was when I saw the most unbelievable thing ever. Seriously. This is the part of the story I really don't expect anyone to believe, but it happened. I have proof.

Maddie dropped back into the trench behind the alligator. She landed and fell down to her knees. Then she reared up and lurched toward the alligator, grabbing for the metal rod that was stuck in her side. I wanted to shout for her to run the other way, but before I could, she yanked the metal stake out of her body.

I can still remember the sound of her scream. I think everyone in the entire Okefenokee Wildlife Refuge heard it.

The metal came out in a gush of blood and puss, and I saw its long, sharp end. I tried to scramble backward, but I couldn't. The alligator opened that horrible mouth full of teeth and clamped down on my shoe. I'm sure my scream was nearly as loud as Maddie's. I struggled to pull my wrecked foot free. It felt like my ankle was in a paper shredder.

I blinked, and Maddie stood over the alligator. With another piercing scream, she raised the sharp metal rod up and brought it down. The blade sunk into the alligator's head, behind its eyes, making it hitch and pause for a second.

Only for a second, though. The gator opened its jaws and then clamped down. I felt those sharp teeth pop through my skin in more places than I care to remember.

Maddie pulled the piece of metal back up and drove it down into the beast's skull again. This time, it gurgled, shuddered, and was motionless. I felt the pressure of the alligator's jaws slacken.

It was dead.

I pulled my ruined foot out of the thing's mouth, and watched as my sister sort of fell over onto her side. The metal thing she'd been carrying in her body for the last day stood straight up in the alligator's skull, like a flagpole marking some newly claimed piece of land.

My foot, covered in blood, felt red-hot, but somehow, I crawled my way over to Maddie. I had to.

"Maddie," I whispered, shaking her limp body. "C'mon, Maddie. Wake up, wake up."

But she wasn't moving.

I heard the splashing and shouts of rescue workers behind me as I put my arms around my crazy, unconscious sister.

My sister had saved my life. I couldn't understand how she'd found the strength to do it, but she had saved my life.

CHAPTER
13

I don't recall much about the workers pulling us out of the muddy trench or anything after that. But I do remember being on the helicopter, about to fly to Folkston, Georgia, the location of the nearest hospital. In the meantime, one of the EMTs at the site did a decent job wrapping up my shredded foot and ankle.

When he was done, I knelt next to Maddie, who was lying down while another medic pressed a towel against her side. I told the guy I'd take over with the towel since we were getting ready to take off for the hospital, and the small helicopter couldn't carry all of us. I mean, I'm no medical guy and no hero, but I knew I could hold a stupid towel on my sister's wound at least, for however long it took. He showed me how much pressure to put on it, and we were up in the air.

I'd never been in a helicopter, but it wasn't like I was there to enjoy the ride. I kept looking at Maddie, waiting for her to open her eyes, for her to say something or show me any other sign of life. It took forever to get to the hospital.

I don't know what they did to Maddie once we got into the emergency room, but they took me to a different area and worked on my foot. I had a bunch of different lacerations on my ankle and puncture wounds all over. I ended up with more stitches than I could count and was told I was awfully lucky not to lose my foot.

I kept asking about Maddie, but they kept telling me they'd check and get back to me. Everyone seemed to say that, which I was sure meant she was dead.

One of the nurses told me that my dad was on his way and would be arriving in a few hours. That gave me a ton of time to lay there by myself and think. The way I figured it, the hospital people didn't want to be the ones to tell me that

Maddie was dead, so they were going to have my dad break the news.

I wondered about things. If we had done something different, would we both have lived? I didn't know. It's not like I'm a survival expert or anything.

I tried to imagine what it would be like not having Maddie around. I'd never have to hear her complain about stuff ever again or listen to her laugh at one of those dumb TV shows she watches. I thought about my mom back in Madison. She would just have gotten the news of our rescue and was probably on her way to see us, too. I wondered how she would feel when she learned Maddie hadn't made it. What would it feel like to lose your daughter?

I started to cry.

It sucked.

A lot.

CHAPTER
14

I must've fallen asleep while crying my dumb head off, because sometime that night, a nurse woke me up. She had an empty wheelchair by the side of my bed.

"Did you want to see your sister?"

I didn't know what to say. Was I going to have to see her in the morgue?

"Where is she?"

"Right next door," the nurse said, smiling. It actually looked like a real smile, not just the kind people have when they feel bad for you, but even so, I didn't want to get my hopes up. I let her help me into the wheelchair and roll me over to room C1141.

When I went into the room, my dad was there, sitting by Maddie's side. He was holding her hand.

"Dad?" I asked, as the nurse moved me to the other side of her bed. "Is she—?"

"Hey, pal," he said softly. "Glad to see you woke up finally. Maddie's fine. She's doing okay."

And just like that, my sister turned her head and looked at me. She still looked rough but not nearly as bad as she had out in the swamp.

"Drew," she whispered, managing a weak smile.

I held Maddie's other hand, a little more gently than I had on the airplane, during those terrifying moments before we plummeted to the ground.

"Thank you," I said to Maddie. "I'd be dead if you hadn't—"

"Don't be stupid, Drew. I'm alive because of you," she interrupted. It was just like my sister. She always had to argue.

Before she left the room, the nurse told us again how very lucky we were. Maddie and I were pretty badly beat up. Maddie had almost died, and I had almost lost a foot. But Maddie was still alive. I had two feet. Dad was with us, and Mom would be there soon, too. For just a little while, our family was going to be together in the same place again.

My dad told us how he'd heard about the crash while waiting at the airport and feared the worst. When the reports came back that there were no survivors, he said he felt as though his whole world had collapsed around him. He said we were the most important people in his life, and he didn't know how he could ever live without us.

I guess that's what it's like when you have kids. I hadn't realized we meant that much to him until just then.

"Were we the only survivors?" I asked my dad, even though I kind of knew the answer.

"Yeah," Dad said. "It sounds like it."

My dad reached under his chair and fumbled for something.

"The crew working at the crash site brought this by," Dad said. He pulled out the cleaned-off piece of metal rod that had almost killed my sister, had killed the alligator, and had saved my life. "They thought the 'gator hunter would want it as a souvenir."

I looked at the thing. It was maybe ten inches long, sharp and jagged on one end where it had broken free from under an airplane seat. Maddie looked at it, too, and then she shook her head.

"I don't want it," she said.

"Don't be so sure," I said. "We're not safely home yet. There are plenty of alligators between here and Florida."

"Oh, shut up," Maddie said, which made me smile. Being all beat up and nearly dead didn't knock the brat out of my little sister. Right then, I knew she'd be okay.

And so, that was pretty much it. We had somehow survived the worst twenty-four hours I can remember. Sure, I had lost my luggage, my phone no longer worked, and my girlfriend would eventually dump me, but really? None of that meant a thing.

I was alive, and so was my sister. That was all that mattered.

FLIGHT DOWN

THOMAS KINGSLEY TROUPE

About the Author

Thomas Kingsley Troupe has always written stuff. Well . . . at least since he was in second grade. Back then it was comic books starring stick people and spaceships. Later it was horror tales and twisted Christmas stories that pretty much ruined the holidays. He also dabbled in writing and directing short films that had audiences laughing one minute and feeling sick another. These days he's the author of more than fifty books for kids. When he's not writing stories, he's fighting fires and hunting ghosts as an investigator with the Twin Cities Paranormal Society. He lives in Woodbury, Minnesota, where he chases his ~~boys~~ monsters around the house. Visit him online at www.thomaskingsleytroupe.com.

Questions to Think About

1. Maddie and Drew are flying from Wisconsin to Florida by themselves. What's the longest trip you've taken by yourself or with only a sibling? It could be a plane trip to another state or just a bike ride to the neighborhood grocery store. Where did you go, and why? What was the trip like? Did you have fun?

2. Drew leads Maddie away from the crash site because of the fire. How might things have been different if they hadn't left? Write a story about what would have happened to Drew and Maddie if they had decided to stay near the spot where they crashed? How would they have survived, and what dangers would they have faced while waiting to be rescued?

3. At the beginning of the story, Drew doesn't seem to like Maddie. He calls her a princess and talks about how he's surprised that she has any friends. But how does Drew *really* feel about his sister? Use examples from the story to explain your answer.

THE DARK LENS

The lens transports Alex to an alternate world filled with ghoulish creatures. When a friend doesn't believe his story about this scary place, Alex agrees to go back—just for a moment. But as night falls, they are trapped in the dark world as creatures lurking in the shadows come out to feed.

The Squadron

Sera has a chance to join an elite group of space pilots. All she needs to do is complete one flight, from the Old World to the New Colonies. But damage to one of her engines sends her off course. She crashes onto a violent dwarf planet with a molten core that is slowly devouring its surface. And that might be the least of her worries.

SPRINT

Filming a sprint car race on the local track, Dylan Clarke captures racer Carlee Martin's fiery accident. The more Dylan replays the video, the more he believes that there's something suspicious about the crash. As he investigates, Dylan discovers that some of Carlee's fellow racers might have wanted to hurt her. And now, they're after him too.

READ MORE FROM 12-STORY LIBRARY
Every 12-Story Library book is available in many formats, including Amazon Kindle and Apple iBooks. For more information, visit your device's store or 12StoryLibrary.com.